FLASH FLOOD
A WEATHER GODS NOVELLA
MELISSA GUNN

MELISSA GUNN

Cover design by Getcovers.com

ISBN 978-0-473-57949-4 (Paperback)

ISBN 978-0-473-57951-7 (epub)

ISBN 978-0-473-57952-4 (Kindle)

ISBN 978-0-473-57953-1 (pdf)

ISBN 978-0-473-57950-0 (Hardcover)

ISBN 9780473579548 (Audiobook)

CONTENTS

AUTHOR'S NOTE

This is the first novel in the Weather Gods series. If you haven't already done so, join my mailing list at www.melissagunn.com to get updates on the series, new releases, and book promotions.

This book is written in New Zealand English, so expect more 's's and 'u's than you might be used to.

It is set in an alternative near-future world much like ours, which is experiencing the effects of climate change, but also has demigods, shifters and other supernaturals.

This is a work of fiction. Please never, ever try to swim in a flash flood!

CHAPTER ONE

Tammy hated getting wet. So it was deeply annoying that she lived in England. That meant nothing but wet, wet wet, all winter and most of the summer.

So unfair. If only we were better off, we could move somewhere warm and dry. If travel abroad was still a thing. Climate change sucks Thor's hairy armpits. Especially since there's more rain here because of it.

Worse still, her inherited demigoddess powers seemed to be bound up with water - not that she knew what she could do with those powers. So far it was just additional misery in the rain.

The rain pelted down on Tammy as she hurried home from school. Large, chilly drops had already soaked through her thin jacket - inadequate for winter, not school regulation, either, but the best she had this year - and splashed off her hood as she tilted her head forward in a pointless attempt to avoid getting even soggier. Rain bounced off the potholed asphalt, soaking her feet. The close-packed stone houses in this area offered nothing in the way of shelter when the downpour was so determined. She hurried past the local pub before she risked a glance behind her. Her little sister Freya was dawdling a good twenty metres back, as usual. She hated having to see her sister home. It meant she had to spend longer in the rain, walking from her own school to Freya's before heading home. And having a little sister around made it practically impossible to make inroads on her relationship with the cute guy at the school she'd joined this term. She pondered the problem as she paused under a leafless street tree for the meagre shelter it provided. Could she see Freya back to their house then leave again? Probably not, Freya was sure to tell their Mum.

"Hurry up, Freya. I'm soaked," called Tammy. Freya didn't appear to hear her. The wind picked up at that moment, shaking yet more droplets from the tree. At least half the water made its way down the back of her neck. Tammy shuddered.

Water. Ugh.

Each droplet felt like it burned as it hit her skin. She was mostly over flinching from the rain by now, but it still wasn't a pleasant experience.

Maybe it's something to do with unrealised power? But I'm supposed to have power over water, not the other way around, at least that's what Mum says. I wish she had more of a clue. As it is I have to rely on being drip-fed - ugh, water again - tips from Dad, and he's got a totally different type of power to me. Wine gods and water goddesses are like, polar opposites.

That made it all the more puzzling that she'd ended up with a water association. Her Mum was all about plants, although her declared heritage was from Freya, goddess of beauty, fertility and such. *She* claimed that plant growth was part of fertility, but Tammy wasn't convinced. Fertility had to be more interesting than just plants.

Also, I can't believe Mum named my sister after a goddess and not me. Not cool.

Dad was unarguably a wine god - or so he always claimed as he sauntered off to sell more of the stuff. And who knew what Freya would turn out to have. But none of that power was something she could talk about with school-friends. Half of them weren't fully human either, but no-one talked about it. Not out loud, anyway. There was too much chance of outing yourself to a full-human, or to someone who didn't know they were a demi. Or worse, to someone who would exploit your power. And humans had long since proven themselves more vicious even than trolls, if once they discovered someone in their midst was different. She snorted to herself at the thought. Thor's hammer! Half of the so-called humans probably qualified as sub-human given their behaviour, and that didn't even include the troll descendants. Look at the way they treated Tammy, as soon as they found out she had 'accommodations' for her dyslexia. No chance she'd ever let them know she was a demigoddess; she'd be torn apart. Or ridiculed forever, which would be worse.

She pulled the hood of her useless jacket further over her face, put her head down and splashed on through the rain.

No point in waiting for Freya, she's bound to get distracted by some plant or stray cat or something. She knows the way home, anyway.

If there had been a stray dog, Tammy would be distracted too. Tammy loved the idea of owning a creature that would actually follow her commands. But every time she begged for one, her parents refused. Too much work, they said. Too expensive.

One day, I'll get a dog of my own, and they won't be able to say anything about it.

Ducking into the slight shelter provided by a house close to the road, Tammy glanced back. Freya *had* paused, beside the town's most obviously abandoned house, a tumbledown dump that had attracted more waste material than seemed possible. Old windows, fallen tiles, ancient black plastic rubbish sacks bulging obesely round the middle, even an extra door that someone had thrown away leaned up against its crumbling exterior. Weedy trees had begun to grow up through cracks between the pavement and the house. Freya was peering down the narrow strip of overgrown pathway that led past the ruined house to a small river that ran through the town.

"Freya! Don't stop, or I'll drown in this rain!"

Freya looked around, startled by Tammy's yell.

"There's water at the end of the lane," she called back.

"I don't care, I just want to get dry. Come *on,*" Tammy said.

Freya cast another doubtful look towards the path, but obediently hurried to catch up with her sister.

"What made you look down there, anyway?" Tammy asked curiously, less stressed now that they were underway again. Soon they'd be home, out of the rain. Assuming the roof wasn't leaking again.

"I thought I heard something. Like an animal, I mean."

"You must have been imagining things. Any sensible animal would be hiding somewhere dry. Like we should be."

"I don't mind the rain. It's better than being too hot," Freya said.

Tammy shuddered.

"Give me heat any time. I can't believe Mum moved here from a country that actually has *droughts*. What was she thinking?"

"You'd know more about that than me. Mum never has time to talk to me. She's always working," Freya complained.

"So, you'd prefer to be the big sister who gets blamed for everything? I'm happy to swap. You be the big sister." Tammy felt bad about the sarcasm that dripped from her voice, though she didn't modulate her tone. It wasn't Freya's fault she was the little sister and totally annoying. "Mum doesn't tell me anything, anyway. Except to look after you and be quick about it. I never get to have a life, it's all about you."

Freya stopped walking and stared at the ground, obviously trying not to cry.

"Oh, get over it, Freya. It's just that I never get any time to myself. I'm a teenager now, I'm supposed to be gaining my independence and figuring out who I'm going to be, not being a free babysitter."

Active waterworks from Freya. That wasn't good. Tammy would be bound to get the blame if anyone reported the incident. Time for a quick intervention. She hastened the step or two back to Freya and gave her a hug.

"It's OK, Frey-Frey. I just hate this rain. It's been raining a week now, and I can't even go outside without feeling like I'm being scalded."

"What do you mean scalded? It's freezing out here." Freya shivered dramatically in demonstration.

"I mean the rain hurts. It feels like it burns me. It's been like this for the last year. Worse this week. It sucks. Especially in winter."

Freya looked at Tammy with wide-open eyes and mouth, the expression giving her a sudden resemblance to their Dad.

"Why didn't you say anything?" she asked.

"Don't look at me like that, I'm not a bug. And just you wait, you might get the same thing when you start getting your powers." Tammy walked a little faster, turning the corner onto the street which led to the bridge over the river. Once they were over that, they'd be almost home. Out of this misery. "I didn't say anything because there's nothing you can do."

"But when I start to get my powers? Will it hurt me too?" Freya's worried voice cut through the sound of the rain.

"How would I-" began Tammy. She stopped, aghast, as the sisters came in sight of the bridge. It was quite a low, flat bridge, because the river it crossed was also usually low and flat. But now, brown water covered it, swirling in delicate patterns around the tops of the posts at each end of the bridge, covering the road and lapping at the grassy banks, far higher than its usual course. There was no way home.

CHAPTER TWO

Tammy felt herself start to hyperventilate immediately.

"I've got to get dry. You have no idea how awful I feel," she gasped.

Freya looked bewildered, eyes wider if that were possible, as she gazed at the flooded river.

"What happened, Tammy? How do we get home?" Her voice was small, scared.

Tammy was reminded all over again of the difference in their ages. Whether she liked it or not, she'd have to pull herself together somehow. She took a deep breath, but flinched as a fresh flurry of raindrops hit her bare skin.

"All this rain must have made that dam upriver burst. We'll have to find someone with a boat," she announced.

Never mind that I've never set foot in a boat. I don't even know anyone who owns one.

Tammy looked around rather wildly. With a mixture of relief and embarrassment - stuck by a flooded river with her little sister wasn't her idea of a great dating spot - she saw the class's cutest guy, Hunter, approaching from behind them. She'd been trying to find a way to get him to notice her for *weeks*. Now it seemed she'd have her chance. He saw her looking at him and waved casually. Tammy waved back, feeling a rush of heat advancing from her neck upwards.

Don't blush, Tammy. Not a good look on you. At least the scalding feeling of rain didn't show up on her skin. She'd checked in the mirror when it first started happening.

"Hunter. I didn't know you went this way too."

Hunter looked past Tammy to the river, and his mouth pulled ruefully to one side. A dimple formed on his cheek.

Adorable, thought Tammy, distracted from her rain-induced discomfort. She really should try to get Hunter to focus on her more often.

"I don't usually go this way. But the ford upriver was flooded, so I thought I'd take the bridge. Looks like I'm out of luck. Which way are you headed?" he said.

Tammy waved a hand at the bridge, trying to match his nonchalance.

"That way. But we need a boat."

Hunter nodded, rubbing his chin with his fingers.

"Could be tricky. My family keeps a boat, but it's on the other side of the river. And with a flood, the currents can be difficult to navigate." Confusingly, he smiled, displaying the white teeth that had first attracted Tammy's attention. As she watched, his gaze swivelled from the flooded river to take in Tammy, rivulets of water darkening her blond hair, clothes stuck to her skin, and Freya, shivering in the continued rain and looking particularly waif-like today. Tammy attempted a dazzling return smile, but wasn't sure she actually achieved it. It was hard to appear enticing when she was wet, bedraggled, and in more pain with every raindrop, but she tried.

"Let's wait in the pub for a bit, in case the flood's just temporary," Hunter suggested.

Tammy and Freya's eyes met. They were both well underage for pubs, and surely Hunter was, too. Besides, the chance of encountering their Dad in the pub was too high, and definitely something to be avoided.

"We need to get home," Tammy said firmly. "We can't wait around."

"What's the rush?" Hunter asked. His brown eyes seemed to spark a little as he watched Tammy. She shivered. What did she know of Hunter after all? Not his species, that was certain. When she first arrived at the school, she thought he must be a descendant of Apollo, all sun-browned skin, glossy hair and glowing personality. Now, though, she wasn't sure. He was an avid member of the top football team, which surely wasn't a sun-god sort of thing. They were usually more about being the centre of attention. And now she was up close, his sunny smile seemed a little toothy and his nostrils flared as a stray gust of wind blew damply past her. Her glance snagged on the fine hairs on his face, which were thickening on his chin and jawline. She didn't think he'd had stubble when he first arrived. Was he a were? It shouldn't matter, though. It was nowhere near a full moon, and she'd been in the same class with him all term without incident - either good or bad. She had been a little disappointed she hadn't managed to contrive a good encounter. At least he hadn't gone for any of the other girls - or boys - either. There was still hope.

"Our house is next to the river. I'm worried we might get flooded." True enough, though she'd only thought of it at this moment.

"In that case, I'll help you find a way across. I don't suppose you want to swim it?"

"You suppose right. That water looks like it's been through several dozen farmers' fields. And I don't like swimming, either," Tammy said. She couldn't imagine how much it would hurt to immerse herself in water these days, rain was bad enough. And the less said about showers, the better. She'd taken to using dry shampoo, this last month.

"You have a point about the muddy water." Hunter laughed as though she'd made a particularly good joke.

Tammy forgot her worries about what species he might be and grinned back, feeling the warm glow of being appreciated. Maybe a flood wasn't so bad.

"Tell you what, maybe we can all cross together. The river's usually just a foot deep. So even high as it is, we should be able to deal with it." Hunter's gaze flicked over to Freya. "I guess your friend might be a bit short, though. Maybe a raft's the way."

Tammy found herself nodding, even though the last thing she wanted to do was go rafting on a flooded river.

"Just a moment, I saw something back there that might be useful." Hunter dashed out of sight around the corner. Tammy shifted uncomfortably as she waited.

"Tammy, what is your friend doing?" Freya asked.

"Trying to help us get home. Somehow."

Hunter reappeared at that moment. Tammy stared, rather. On his shoulder, he had balanced what appeared to be a door. After a disoriented moment, she recognised it as the door from the abandoned house. In his other hand he held a sturdy sapling, recently stripped of its branches.

"What's that for?" Tammy wondered aloud.

"A raft. If you don't want to get wet, I can't think of any other way across," Hunter said.

Tammy looked at the door dubiously.

"Are you sure we'll fit? And how would we steer?"

"I'll take you across one at a time. With this pole to steer. Just like punting on the Avon." He raised the sapling in explanation. Hunter sounded confident enough, but Tammy noticed him glancing at the flooded river with a frown on his face.

"Take Freya first, then. She's smaller and lighter," said Tammy. "You're more likely to get her across safely than me." She wasn't sure herself if she was being kind or not. But at least if Freya got across, Tammy would be able to talk to Hunter without a second pair of ears listening in on her all the time. And Freya would be closer to home. Win win.

Freya looked scared, but didn't protest. Hunter took off his bag and pulled out a fur coat, of all things. He held it out to Tammy.

"Here, hold this over you while I get your friend settled."

"She's my sister, not my friend," Tammy corrected automatically, wondering why Hunter hadn't realised that she and Freya were related at once. Especially if he was a were. They were supposed to have an amazing sense of smell. She noticed the hurt on Freya's face and tried not to feel guilty about that, but it was difficult. She took the coat anyway, wondering why on earth Hunter had one in his bag. Fur coats had been out of fashion since before she was born. But where the coat covered her arm, she was suddenly warm, dry and comfortable again. She found herself clutching it with both arms, snuggling her cheek against it. What was this coat, that it made her feel so good? She stroked it wonderingly. A pointed throat-clearing broke her concentration and she looked up, embarrassed to find

Hunter watching her with sharp eyes. Freya had climbed onto the door where Hunter had laid it flat at the edge of the water, and was kneeling on it, holding onto the edges with a white-knuckled grip.

"When you've quite finished cuddling my coat, can you help get this thing launched? I'll take it from front end, if you can steady it to start with." Hunter was crouched next to Freya, holding the door still as the floodwaters attempted to take it downriver.

Tammy twitched her hand guiltily away from the fur.

"Er, yes. I guess. How come you have a fur coat in your bag?" She dropped her bag in order to slip her arms into the coat, buttoning it tightly against the wind, and stepped nervously towards the water. She couldn't imagine how much a whole river of water would hurt her.

"It's an inheritance. My Gran died last week, and my aunt passed it on to me today after school." He rolled his eyes. "Loki knows what I'll do with it, but plunging it into a river probably isn't what Gran had in mind."

"Relatives are so weird sometimes," agreed Tammy, while wondering if his reference to Loki meant he was actually related to that god. Surely not. He never played pranks in class. And he didn't look at all Scandinavian.

"I know, right. Gran used to wear that thing at the beach. I used to pretend she wasn't anything to do with me - and then she'd come and make me sit beside her to build sandcastles or whatever. I can't see myself wearing it, ever. Tell you what. Why don't you keep it? It'd look better on you than it'll look on me."

Tammy hesitated; her hand drawn back to the coat in spite of herself.

"I couldn't take your inheritance."

"Sure, you could. It's a gift. It's only going to gather dust in my wardrobe otherwise. And you look like you need a good coat."

Great, now he's noticed how all my clothes are second-hand. You'd think with two working parents we'd have enough to live on, but no. Maybe if Dad spent less time in pubs, we'd have more money for clothes.

She stroked the coat absently. She'd have to hide it if she took it home. Mum would have a fit if she turned up in fur. On the plus side, Hunter was paying enough attention to her that he had realised she was cold and miserable.

Never mind, figure that out later. Get across the river first.

She took hold of the door, shuddering when her hands of necessity touched the water.

"Are you ready, Freya?"

"I suppose so. What do I do if I fall off?" Freya asked.

Tammy looked doubtfully at the brown, silken eddies that silently swirled in the centre of the river.

"Hope it doesn't happen. And keep your head above water if it does. Your feet will probably touch the ground, at least."

Freya made a face.

"I don't fancy drinking mud."

"So, keep your mouth closed."

Hunter interrupted this dubious sisterly exchange.

"Hold tight, kid. Tammy, I'll stand on the door while you steady it. Ready?" He stepped onto the door, which dipped briefly underwater before he shifted to stand in the middle of it, beside Freya. Setting his sapling into the water on one side, he gave Tammy a nod. "Give us a push to start. We'll be over to the other side in no time."

Chapter Three

Tammy watched Hunter worriedly as he poled his unlikely craft across the swollen river. Each push with the pole propelled them a little way, but also made the door wobble ferociously. Every time it did so, Tammy felt her stomach clench with anxiety.

I hope they get across alright.

Hunter clearly had some experience with boats, but still, they were going downriver faster than they were crossing it. At this rate they'd disappear around the bend before they made it across. Freya was obviously getting concerned too. She kept glancing back at Tammy, mouth forming words that Tammy couldn't interpret. Tammy paced beside the river, avoiding its watery fingers, but trying to keep close to Hunter and Freya. Before long, someone's garden wall blocked her path. She scrambled impatiently over it, trusting that she'd be across the garden before she was noticed.

"You there!"

So much for that.

The voice was an unwelcome intrusion. Tammy spotted its source, a middle-aged man leaning out of a conservatory door with lowered brows. No way she wanted to explain herself to *him*. She sprinted across the garden, dodging empty flower beds, and leaped over the next wall, thankful that it was low enough for her to do so. The last she heard of the angry man was a fading 'Oy!'. But where were Hunter and Freya? Tammy scanned the river for them as she jogged across someone else's garden. Fortunately, no-one seemed to be home here. The river was fuller than ever, breaking out of its banks now. A flicker of movement caught her eye as she was halfway over the next wall. Hunter and Freya were still on the door, closer to the opposite shore but with a couple of metres still to go. Hunter glanced over his shoulder and saw her.

"Nearly there!" he called.

At that moment, something submerged caught at the door, causing it to spin violently around. Freya shrieked. Hunter whipped his pole into the air in a valiant attempt to keep his balance, but after a moment's almost graceful wavering, plunged backwards into the muddy water. The change in weight completely unbalanced the door, and Freya slipped off the other side as it tipped.

"Freya!" Tammy yelled. "Fenris' teeth!"

Tammy half-ran into the muddy current, gritting her teeth as her legs flared with the pain of water. An unexpected hole underfoot took her neck-deep. The force of the current caught the coat, swept her feet from under her and she splashed face-first into the river.

At first, Tammy thought it was the unwanted touch of water all over her that caused the odd sensation. She tried to ignore it, flailing her arms and kicking her feet in an attempt to get her head above water. She couldn't let Freya drown, even if her skin did burn from the water cascading over her. Or was that a crawling, prickling sensation? The lack of air must be getting to her. She felt firm mud beneath her feet and pushed off. Her face burst through the surface a moment later and she gasped reflexively for air. The burning in her lungs eased, but the prickling feeling remained.

It must be that coat. At least I haven't lost it, Hunter would hate me if I lost his Gran's coat just after he got it.

She ignored the prickling as best she could and looked around for Freya. Blinking water out of her eyes, she thought she saw Hunter's form. She took a deep breath and dived under, paddling as best she could in that direction. Swimming seemed to be easier this time. Perhaps she was remembering her long-ago swimming lessons. It was amazing how long one breath lasted, too. Really, she was better at swimming than she'd realised. And the scalding she usually experienced from water had quite gone. If she didn't know she was immersed in a turbid drain of a river, she'd be rather enjoying herself. Tammy twisted and rolled as she swam, just to see how it felt. Glorious. She could hear stones rattling along the bottom of the river-bed, and curious clicking noises. Fish, maybe? But she needed to find Freya. Raising her head above water - so easily - she spotted Freya's water-darkened mousy head just passing under a denuded willow. At least her head *was* above water. Another breath, a quick dive, some underwater bumping around unseen branches, and she was pushing Freya close to the bank. Freya grabbed at the roots of the willow where they dipped into the water and hauled herself out. Her lips were blue with cold and she was coughing. Tammy climbed out after her.

Freya doesn't look like she's in good shape. I guess she's smaller than me, maybe she loses heat faster. But where's Hunter?

Tammy glanced around. Hunter was a few metres downriver, staggering out of the water, but apparently unharmed.

Hmm, not as much of a wet-shirt advert as I expected, Tammy observed. Hunter was skinny under his flattering clothing, ribs showing, yet to fill out. He gave himself a dog-like shake, water spraying off his mid-length hair. *Almost certainly a werewolf. I wonder if he'd respond favourably to a good, firm 'heel'?* She smirked to herself at the thought. *Better not try it just yet. Not until I'm really sure of him. But oh, it's so tempting.*

Tammy was distracted from her musings as Freya, arms wrapped around herself in an attempt to keep warm, turned towards Tammy - and gave a short scream. Freya covered her mouth with her hand, only to remove it to gasp, "Tammy? Is that you? *What happened?*"

"Of course, it's me. How about a thank you for risking water to get you to safety?" Tammy retorted - or tried to. The sound that came out of her mouth was not distinguishable as words. She lifted her own hands. To her horror, she saw that they were covered with dense brown fur.

Tammy touched one hand to her face. It felt normal enough. But when she held it out again, there was that fur. She could see her fingers underneath it, each one encased in a sleek coat more suited for an otter or a seal than a human. Her own nails showed though, still with their usual slightly-pinker-than-school-regulations gloss polish. She felt herself start to hyperventilate again. This was more terrifying than water.

It must be the coat. Just the coat. Don't panic, Tammy.

Freya wasn't helping, looking at her like she was a monster out of some particularly terrifying fairy tale.

Squelching footsteps announced Hunter's arrival at their frozen tableau.

"What do you know, that coat still works. I knew you should have it," he said cheerfully.

Tammy rounded on him furiously.

"What in Frigg's name have you done to me?" she began, before realising that her words still weren't coming out right.

Hunter's dimple was back. His eyes were warm as he looked her up and down.

"You'd make a great addition to our pack," he said. "You turned without even a whimper. Most first-timers scream, not swim. And you smell amazing. I hope you don't mind mixed races. Not everyone is a wolf or a seal."

Tammy found that suddenly, his dimple wasn't nearly as attractive as she'd thought. She reached up to her neck, and to her relief, her questing hands found the front of the coat. She tore it off, ignoring the wrench she felt as it parted ways with her skin, and threw it at Hunter, who caught it reflexively.

"Mixed races is not a problem. The problem is you let this - this *thing* take me over without even a warning!" Tammy's voice was strident, echoing off the brick and stone buildings on this side of the river. Windows creaked open as curious townspeople tried to see what was happening. She didn't care. For a few horrible moments, she'd thought she'd be encased in fur forever. No matter how much better it made water feel, that was *not* going to be her future.

"But I didn't -" began Hunter.

"I thought you were being kind, helping us across this horrible river." She looked behind her at the river, still too close for comfort, and couldn't help but remember that it had felt wonderful.

Never mind how it felt.

"And all with some plan to get me into your *pack,* with a nasty cling-on coat which probably came from some poor selkie your Gran murdered. Well, have I got news for you. I don't need your pack. And I don't need your coat. I'm glad we're on the right side of the river now, but I never want to see you again."

Hunter's face seemed to close in on itself. When he spoke, it was through clenched teeth with suspiciously prominent canines.

"I have been trying to help you. You were cold. I could *smell* your pain. That's why I offered you the coat."

"Yeah, right," sneered Tammy, knowing even as she did so that she was being needlessly antagonistic. Somehow, she couldn't help herself.

"Yeah, right," replied Hunter seriously. "I'm sorry you were surprised by the coat. But it did its job, didn't it? You're not in pain now?"

Tammy belatedly realised that she was standing in the pelting rain with no ill effects.

"No, but I don't see why your coat would have anything to do with it."

"It makes the wearer at home in the water. As you experienced. You looked like you were born to it."

"So, it is some selkie's fur." Tammy shuddered at the thought of wearing someone else's skin. "No thank you. I won't wear someone's stolen identity."

"It's been in my family for generations. It's not like someone went out of their way to trap a selkie. If my aunt is right, it's from an ancestor of mine, not stolen at all. And anyway, we don't need extra fur. That's why I felt comfortable giving it to you."

Tammy rolled her eyes at this inadvertent admission that Hunter was in fact a were. Or maybe a selkie? But that didn't seem to fit his style. He suited his name.

"Yeah, I get that," she said. "You just felt entitled. You and your family probably just run this town, don't you? That's what werepacks do."

Hunter shifted and looked uncomfortable.

"My Dad's on council," he said. "But that's not running it. He was elected."

"And the selkie thing? You're not seals in human clothing, are you?"

"No. At least, not seals. Though I wonder about Gran, now. But I guess you can't smell that like I do."

"You got that right. Thank goodness."

"It's not a curse. Quite the reverse, except in the gym changing rooms."

Tammy was momentarily side-tracked from her ire by the horrible thought of smelling *more* in the changing rooms.

Don't get distracted, Hunter was trying to rope you into his pack without even asking.

"I don't need to know what your over-sensitive nose tells you. More than it should, I'm guessing," she said. "You probably know all the trolls in town."

Hunter shook his head – though Tammy noticed he exactly didn't deny her accusation.

"That's why I mentioned mixed races. Some people round here take issue with our mixed heritage, as though anyone in this country is purely one thing or another." Hunter was almost spitting his words.

I sure touched a nerve there.

"Who cares what bigots think? But I still don't want to wear fur," Tammy said.

Freya, who had seemed to be huddled into a sort of hypothermic trance, watching Hunter and Tammy argue, suddenly spoke up.

"Tammy, can we go home now? If anyone around here does have issues with race, they know all about it now. And I can hear a siren. Someone must have seen something."

Freya's words, accompanied by the distant wail of a siren - police, fire or ambulance, Tammy couldn't remember the difference - brought

Tammy out of her haze of rage, and for the first time she realised that they weren't in some isolated spot, but rather three doors down from a convenience store, surrounded by houses and listening ears. She cringed internally, but did her best to put on a display of bravado.

"I'm going home. Now. Freya needs to get dry. So do I."

And I'm going to hope there aren't any repercussions from Hunter discussing his heritage with me on the high street.

There was a small noise, not much more than a rustle of wet twigs, behind her. A large, brown and golden dog was standing there, staring at her intently.

Tammy felt her heart race, uncertain what this off-leash beast was going to do. However, after a moment it glanced at Hunter, growled, then turned and trotted upriver.

Hunter looked at Tammy sadly, his frustration gone as quickly as it had come.

"Farewell, then," he said formally.

Fenris' teeth, what's got into him? He was inviting me to join his family a few minutes ago. Now he's acting like he'll never see me again.

Tammy shrugged, realising as she did so that she'd left her school bag on the other side of the river.

Oh well, it's not like I was going to do any homework, anyway. I just hope it's still there tomorrow, or whenever this flood goes down.

"See you round," she said carelessly, as though she hadn't just had a life-changing experience. Taking Freya's hand, she tugged her sister in the direction of home.

CHAPTER FOUR

Tammy was relieved to find that their house hadn't been flooded, at least not yet. She and Freya did have to slosh through a few inches of water to get to the front door, but the flood had only covered the road so far.

"Why were you mean to Hunter?" Freya asked her as they closed the door behind them.

Tammy wheeled round halfway through tugging off her damp jacket.

"Seriously? I wasn't mean to him; he was the one who tried to make me into a Loki-cursed selkie. Without even a warning."

"He probably didn't expect you to jump into the water," suggested Freya mildly.

Tammy kicked her jacket into a corner, knowing she'd have to pick it up later, but not caring right now.

"He shouldn't have capsized with you on board then. And he should have told me anyway. There was me wanting to get to know him better!" Tammy stomped into the kitchen to make herself a warm drink.

Freya, who had hung up her own coat, ducked into the front room to wrap herself in a blanket. Her voice floated back to Tammy.

"Would you really want to know a werewolf better, Tammy?"

Tammy thought a moment before answering.

"No more or less than any other cute guy, I guess."

"The fur thing doesn't worry you?"

What is Freya getting at? She's not usually preoccupied with werewolves.

"Not if I don't have to wear it." A thought struck her and she bounded back out of the kitchen, abandoning her drink. "Forget about werewolves, Freya. I've just realised I can have a proper shower again!" As Tammy headed for the bathroom, she almost missed Freya's muttered words.

"But you *were* wearing fur."

Some time later, splashing sounds heralded the return of Tammy and Freya's Mum, Danae. She stood in the hall to lever off her shoes and hang up her coat, uttering groaning noises. Tammy ignored the noises as normal background noise, until Danae stuck her head into the front room.

"I hope you didn't have any trouble getting home, girls," Danae said. "There's water right up to the front step."

Tammy and Freya exchanged glances.

"Well," Freya began.

"We got home all right," said Tammy quickly, before Freya could say anything more.

"That's good. I'm going to check the news. I hope that river's not rising still. I've put some towels at the front door just in case." Bustling out, she didn't seem to notice the hissed conversation that broke out behind her.

"Aren't you going to tell her what about the river?" asked Freya.

"Not happening. And don't you either. We'd be grounded till Ragnarök."

"Lucky that's not a thing, then," said Freya. She fell silent as their Mum's footsteps passed by in answer to a knock at the door.

They could hear an indistinct, low voice, interrupted at intervals by their mother's stressed tones. She reappeared a minute later, running her hands through her hair in a harassed manner.

"Girls, pack a bag. That was a policeman. Apparently, we may have to evacuate."

"But Mum!" they exclaimed together.

"I know, it's the last thing any of us wants to do. I don't even know when your father will get back. He's still off on that sales trip. Just… just get some warm clothes, maybe a torch or something. Just in case." She left the room abruptly, striding upstairs, presumably to pack her own bag.

Probably packing her favourite seeds.

Tammy drummed her fingers on the arm of the threadbare couch.

"Can I borrow your bag, Freya?" she asked suddenly. "I left mine behind."

"That's not fair, your clothes take up more space than mine," protested Freya.

"I'll carry it if we have to leave," Tammy said.

It was a long evening, an exhausting mixture of nervous tension and tedium keeping everyone awake as they waited up in case they were ordered to leave. Freya insisted on packing her favourite books before letting Tammy stuff any clothes into her schoolbag. There was barely room for the few things Tammy had, and none for her damp uniform.

"We'd better not have to leave. I need my uniform on Monday, you know," grumped Tammy.

"So do I," said Freya. "But I prefer my books to my uniform."

"I don't prefer my uniform, if that's what you're implying. I just don't want to be sent home for not wearing it. You don't know what it's like at high school."

"So why did you leave your bag behind?" asked Freya.

"To rescue you, obvs! How about a bit more gratitude?"

Freya huddled in on herself.

"I was fine. Mostly."

CHAPTER FIVE

Several hours passed without an evacuation order, although Tammy and Freya had been herded into bucket duty by their mother, Danae, when the towels at the door became uselessly sodden. If Danae noticed Tammy's sudden indifference to water, she didn't comment. They'd moved all the pot plants, cushions and blankets upstairs by then, along with what food was in the kitchen. The lights had gone off some time ago, and they were making do with one torch and some tealights that Freya had found in the bottom drawer of the kitchen.

"I wish we'd got that solar upgrade the council was offering," muttered Danae.

"Mum, it's dark and raining. It wouldn't matter if we did have an upgrade," Tammy said, tossing yet another bucket of water out the front window with a splash. It didn't make much difference to the water sloshing around the hall.

"I'm hungry, Mum," complained Freya.

"Eat some cereal, then. That doesn't need heating," Danae said. Freya morosely put down the bowl she'd been using as a bucket and squelched upstairs, presumably to find the cereal.

"I suppose there's enough cereal for us all, Mum?" Tammy said.

"Let's hope so," said her Mum grimly.

The evacuation order came in the middle of the night, the policeman hammering at their door again, wearing angling waders that went up to his thighs. This time he had a wet dog in tow, water dripping off its floppy ears and making its long coat cling to its rather skinny sides. Looking at it blearily from behind Danae, Tammy wondered if it was just a dog, or if was really a werewolf. Her Mum had told her about weres, and how to spot them in human form, but had been hazy on differentiating a shifted were from a regular animal. This one just looked wet and miserable, transferring its gaze from Danae to her. It gave a small whine, and the hint of a tail-wag, and the policeman jerked its leash till it subsided. It looked like just the sort of animal Tammy would love to own.

I wouldn't pull a dog around like that.

"Do we really have to go?" asked Danae.

"Afraid so, ma'am. It's not safe to stay. Electricity has been cut off to reduce the chance of fires, but this water is likely to be contaminated, and it's rising still. Best to go now before things get worse."

"Oh."

Tammy reflected that her Mum was not at her best at night.

"Where are we supposed to go? What should we take?" she asked.

The bright beam of light from the policeman's torch skewered Tammy in place. Blinking at the unexpected assault of brightness, she struggled to see his face, but she fancied his eyes widened a little as he looked at her. Did his nostrils flare, too? She shivered. But his answer was straightforward.

"The church on that little rise just outside town is above the floodwaters. We're sending everyone there that can fit."

"And if it's full?" Tammy asked.

"We'll cross that bridge when we come to it. It could be there's space at the big house. In either case, you'll need food and warm clothing."

The big house was a manor well outside of town. Tammy wasn't sure who lived there, but it was certainly on high ground.

"If you'll excuse me, ladies, I need to get the rest of this street notified. You'll need to be leaving in the next fifteen minutes. I'll be checking back to make sure everyone's out." The policeman turned away to slosh to the next house in the street, torchlight gleaming off the brown, watery flatness which had replaced the usual road and grassy river frontage. His dog looked back at Tammy and whined again before trailing after him.

Is there something familiar about its eyes? Tammy wondered. *Impossible to tell in the dark.*

Danae closed the door on the unedifying scene and slumped against it briefly before rallying.

"Well then, Tammy. You'd better go collect your bags. Wake up Freya." Danae added wearily, "I don't fancy a crowd. I wish we could stay here. Even if it meant cold baked beans and cereal for the duration."

Tammy was of the opinion that a crowd in a warm space would be preferable to that fate, especially since they couldn't heat the house now.

But no-one ever pays attention to what I want. At least I got a hot shower before the water was cut off. Best shower in a year.

And she hadn't reacted to all the nasty water leaching into the house from the floods. Maybe she was coming into her powers properly at last.

Or maybe Hunter's coat has left some sort of mark on me. Ugh.

She shuddered.

Although reclaiming water is probably worth it.

Freya had trailed upstairs to curl up in bed some hours ago. She didn't take kindly to being woken. While she muttered, Tammy took the opportunity to squeeze a few more of her own things into the outside pockets of Freya's bag, wishing she hadn't left her own bag behind, no matter what she'd told her sister. Who knew how long they'd be away from home?

Chapter Six

The church was full. A matronly woman at the door turned them away kindly but firmly.

"Sorry loves, we just can't fit another body in here. We're bursting at the seams already. You'll have to go on to the big house. You know where that is?"

Danae nodded, but said;

"Can't we just go home?"

"Oh, I wouldn't do that, love. It's not safe, you know. Don't worry, they'll have room at the big house."

As they trudged away, Tammy noticed another family arriving. It looked like they'd have company wherever they went. She kicked at the puddles, as she'd not done in a year.

"Mum, if I have water abilities, shouldn't I be able to do something about this flood?" she asked.

"It's not that simple, Tammy. Your abilities are just beginning to mature. We don't know yet what you can do. And the waters have personalities of their own, you can't just tell them what to do like you do Freya."

"I don't do what she says anyway," said Freya.

Tammy ignored her and kept walking and splashing. *Typical adult response. It's always 'you're not old enough yet'.*

It didn't help that she'd had to put her wet anorak back on, and that wasn't combining well with a long walk in the drizzly dark. She took out her irritability on the puddles.

"How do you know about water, anyway, Mum? That's not your power, is it?" Tammy asked.

She felt, rather than saw, her Mum shaking her head.

"Everything has personality, Tammy. Remember that. Water spirits and deities inhabit rivers and lakes, and they are affected by their surroundings as much as anyone."

"So, floodwater has the personality of a big wet blanket?" suggested Tammy.

Danae laughed unexpectedly.

"I suppose so. I'm more familiar with plant spirits. But I doubt that water deities in floodwaters are a good first spirit for anyone to meet," she said.

Tammy considered this. She hadn't been thinking of water spirits when she splashed into the water after Freya. But under that flat surface, the water had been anything but boring.

I may have to explore this water thing further. When Mum's not watching.

They reached the big house just before it seemed that Freya would collapse from exhaustion. Tammy didn't want to admit that she was just as tired. She felt unspeakably awkward approaching the large house from its curving, puddle-flecked driveway. It had a light on by the door, so at least they were probably expecting people.

It was worse when the door opened. A man who vaguely reminded Tammy of Hunter stood there in his dressing gown, looking stuffy and upper class despite opening his own door.

"Yes? Can I help you?" he asked.

Tammy cringed.

He doesn't sound like he's expecting anyone. This is just as embarrassing as I thought it would be.

"They sent us here from the church," Danae explained. "It was full."

"Botheration. We'll be up the rest of the night getting people settled in. Ah well. Come in, since you're here."

The family trooped in, feeling small and grubby in the tall-ceilinged hall. A flurry of barking erupted from one of the closed doors nearby.

"Keep it down in there," the man yelled.

He turned to Danae.

"I hope you don't mind dogs. We have a fair few here. I'm Mayor Hovart, as you probably know. Looks like I've been called upon to do my bit for the town, eh?" He chuckled, clearly inviting them to appreciate his humour. Danae looked like she didn't know what to say. Tammy didn't, either. She just wanted to go home to her own bed.

"Thank you for having us," Danae said. "I hope we'll be able to head back to our own house when it's daylight."

"Well, I don't know about that. The weather reports are pretty nasty, I hear. However, we'll hope for the best. For now, I'll put you and your girls in here." He swung open a heavy wooden door near the end of the hall and gestured for them to go in. They did so, hesitantly. Inside, the room was chilly, uncarpeted. A wide bed took up most of the space, and an unlit fireplace contained dried flowers.

"Make yourself at home in here. You'll find the conveniences across the hall. Any questions? No? Good. I'll get back to bed while I can."

The door closed behind him with a hollow thud, which provoked a further outburst of barking.

"We *are* going home tomorrow, aren't we Mum?" asked Freya.

"Yeah, I think I just figured out that that's Hunter's Dad. It would be super-embarrassing to stay here, Mum," added Tammy.

I probably shouldn't tell her we are in a house full of weres, right? Maybe she knows anyway.

Danae did look more hollow-eyed than a mere night walk would account for, however soggy.

"I would be extremely happy to go home in the morning, girls. Meanwhile, it looks like we're stuck here, so we may as well get some sleep. At least we've a bed, that's more than we would have had at the church. Get your wet things off. We'll have to share the bed, but I expect that will keep us warmer anyway."

CHAPTER SEVEN

The next morning was just as tricky as Tammy had imagined. When they emerged from their room, bleary-eyed after a poor night's sleep sharing a too-crowded unfamiliar bed, a large dog with long gold-brown fur and a black saddle leaped up at Tammy, tail wagging as it licked at her face. Hunter himself appeared behind the dog.

"Get down, Diana," he said in an irritated voice. "They'll think you have no manners."

The dog gave Hunter a resentful look, but retreated, nails clicking on the wooden floor as it walked the short distance down the hall to the kitchen, which was announcing its presence with strong cooking smells.

Hunter looked warily at Tammy, but addressed himself to Danae.

"Sorry about Diana, she's still pretty young. You're to have breakfast with us in the dining room. A few other families came in last night, but they're mostly not up yet. This way."

"I didn't realise you lived here," Tammy said as she followed resentfully.

"Yes. Well. This is my family's house. The boatshed is down by the river." He looked at her sideways. "But I suppose you're not interested in that now."

"You suppose right," agreed Tammy in frosty tones.

Hunter opened the door to the dining room in silence.

'Breakfast' was an understatement, Tammy thought. Large trays of scrambled eggs, various types of meat, and the almost inevitable baked beans were laid out on a sideboard in warming dishes. The mayor from last night and a couple of tall, muscular looking women were already in the dining room, eating from heavily laden plates. The women glanced up as the door opened, but quickly returned their attention to their food. While Tammy and her family were still hovering indecisively, the women cleared their plates, then arose and left the room, leaving the dirty dishes on the table.

Hoping she was doing the right thing, Tammy picked up a plate and served herself some beans and a piece of toast. Although the beans were warm, the toast was cold and floppy. Tammy grimaced at the feel of it. Freya and Danae followed her lead, serving themselves beans. Hunter followed them, heaping bacon and eggs onto his plate and piling toast beside that.

"Don't you want anything else?" he asked. They all shook their heads.

"Suit yourselves." He shrugged and pulled out a chair. The mayor cleared his throat loudly and Hunter sighed and pulled out chairs for Tammy, Freya and Danae. Tammy couldn't figure out his attitude now.

Sure, it's super-awkward being here after I said I didn't want to see him again, but it's not like I wanted to come. Doesn't he know that?

"Are there many other evacuees here?" Tammy asked Hunter, trying to avoid an uncomfortable silence.

He looked at her uncertainly, glancing at his busily masticating father before answering.

"Just a couple. Most people went to the church."

"Which we were turned away from? Hmm."

"Is there any news about the flood?" Danae asked quickly.

Again, Hunter looked to his father as though for permission before answering.

"I think the water was still rising, last I heard. But I haven't checked since six this morning."

Mayor Hovart swallowed a large mouthful and cleared his throat.

"I very much doubt that your home will be fit for returning to today. It's been raining all night. No reason for the floods to have gone down yet."

Tammy looked suspiciously at him. There was something she didn't like about Hunter's Dad.

"I'd like to check myself," Danae insisted. "I have plants to keep alive."

The expression on the mayor's face suggested he didn't consider plants a major concern.

"The local constable is due to report in to me shortly. Why don't you wait and ask him?" he suggested. "But first, you should have more to eat. Have some bacon. Or a steak. There's plenty to go round."

"We have enough, thanks," Danae said. Freya looked like she was having trouble controlling her expression. None of their family ate meat. The mayor's brow furrowed and his face grew red. He seemed about to say more. Tammy found herself noticing the size of his teeth, bared in what was probably meant to be a smile. Out of the corner of her eye she saw Hunter step quietly towards the door. When he saw her looking, he inclined his head in invitation.

"Excuse me, I've just got to er, go," Tammy announced.

Freya looked at her in surprise. She'd only eaten a few of her beans, poking them around her plate with her fork.

"Stay here, Freya," Danae said. "We'll stick together. Tammy, come right back, please."

"Yes, Mum," agreed Tammy pleasantly. No harm in making it seem that she was doing as she was told.

Back in the hall, Hunter was waiting. He gestured for her to follow, and led the way to the kitchen. Despite the cooking smells, no-one was present in there. A windowed door on the far side of the room promised to lead outside. Diana, the enthusiastic dog from earlier, leapt up from a large cushion near the Aga on one side and followed them to the door, looking up at Hunter pleadingly.

"Oh, all right then," he said.

Diana leaped joyfully through the door and dashed off into the drizzle.

"I've always wanted a dog like that," Tammy commented as they stepped outside after her.

"Really?" Hunter sounded disbelieving.

"Yes. I like dogs. Unlike the rest of my family."

"I'm not sure that Diana's quite what you're after in a dog," Hunter said.

"Why's that?"

A young girl – about Freya's age, Tammy thought – was returning through the damp shrubs, pulling down a dress as she went. She shared Hunter's colouring, which, now Tammy came to think about it, was rather like that of Diana-the-dog.

"Oh."

"Hey Diana. Did Dad ground you again?" Hunter asked.

Diana looked sideways.

"Maybe?"

"I suppose he caught you sneaking out. You know what he's like, why do you keep trying?"

"I wanted to see what the floods are like. Everyone's making such a fuss over them. There's no reason I can't go look. Uncle Archie went. Aunt Fiona went. Even you went. Why shouldn't I?"

Hunter led Diana and Tammy further into the bushes before answering.

"Because every time he catches you, he puts more restrictions on the rest of us. He's been worse than ever since Gran died, and you know it."

Diana pouted, and Tammy reflected that she'd never seen Freya do that. Maybe her little sister wasn't the worst.

"It's not fair," Diana said.

"I know, but just hang in there a bit longer. Otherwise, we'll all be in the doghouse."

Diana groaned.

"You always think you're so clever with that joke. I bet your friend doesn't even get it." She looked at Tammy with narrowed eyes, as though to assess the effect of this pronouncement. Tammy decided that the best thing to do was ignore it.

"Tell you what, Diana, how about you go check the flood levels, while you're out here," Hunter suggested.

"You just want some time alone with your *girl*friend," Diana accused.

"Sure, you got me. But this is also the only way you'll get to see the floods. Besides, I'd trust your report more than Uncle Archie's. I know you'll tell me what's really going on."

"Oh, all right." Diana bounded off into a bush, which lurched around for a few moments, rustling wetly. Instead of a girl, the dog Tammy had first seen in the hall emerged from the bush.

Hunter rolled his eyes.

"Diana has no sense of discretion." He turned back to Tammy. "Look, I'm sorry you got sent here. I mean, I wanted to see more of you and all, but then my Dad got wind of that yesterday and decided he had to check out your family. He's pretty strict like that."

"You mean we didn't have to leave our house?" Tammy's tone was accusing.

"Um. We'll see what Diana has to say. But there was flooding outside your house last night. My Uncle Archie's the constable in town, he was doing the rounds and took me with him…" Unexpectedly, colour rose in his cheeks and he looked away from Tammy.

Was he the dog with the policeman last night? And he didn't say anything.

"Wow, and I thought my parents were controlling. Your family sounds unbelievable!"

"Yeah. They take that whole wolf hierarchy thing pretty seriously. Which is crazy, because you saw Diana. Um, and me. We're totally not wolves."

Tammy burst out laughing, despite being appalled at the situation she and her family were in.

"Not wolves at all. What are you, farm dogs?"

Hunter's colour increased.

"Like I told you yesterday, we're a mix. Some wolf, sure. But my Dad's got a thing about that. I thought I could do what I wanted with my life, hang out with who I like. But after yesterday and this morning? Well, I don't know what to think anymore. It might not be safe for you here. Especially since you're not weres like us at all."

"Why should we be?" Tammy retorted.

"No reason, as far as I'm concerned. But Dad…"

"Is racist?"

"Er. Maybe? He wants to restore our aristocracy or something."

"That is so weird."

"No, it's not. He's just got strong ideas. And when you didn't eat everything at breakfast, that really upset Dad. He's big on people accepting his hospitality."

Tammy shook her head slowly.

"You know, between that selkie coat thing and your Dad, your family is all kinds of messed up. Which is a shame, because you're kind of cute. But as things are..." She patted his arm regretfully. "Sorry. Nothing doing."

Hunter's face was definitely dimple-less. No laughter today.

"Yeah. I know. I just wanted to get you out here so I could explain. Apologise, I guess. Because if Dad decides he doesn't like your family, he'll stick at nothing to move you on."

Tammy felt her insides clench with tension.

"But – he can't do that. It's not his town."

"As far as he's concerned, it is. Just be careful, alright? I had thought we might have had a chance at something special. But I don't want to see you or your family hurt because of me."

Tammy opened her mouth to retort that her family could look after themselves, but Diana came racing back through the shrubs just then, tongue lolling as she bounded towards them. She repeated her dive into a bush, and crawled out very damp and twiggy and human-shaped, wearing another short, knit dress that had seen better days.

"It's almost all gone," she announced. "But there's mud everywhere, and it stinks! I only just missed being seen by Uncle Archie, though. He was putting yellow caution tape all along that row of houses by the river."

"You take too many risks, Diana. I hope he didn't smell you. Get back into the kitchen now, before anyone *does* see you," Hunter said.

Diana dashed back towards the house. Tammy stared after her, fists balling up.

"*We* live in the row of houses by the river," she said, in a voice she hardly recognised as her own.

"Yes. I saw last night. We'd better get your family out now. So you can retrieve anything you need."

His voice was even heavier than when he had farewelled her yesterday.

Tammy started walking towards the house without saying anything. What else was there to say, after all?

53

CHAPTER EIGHT

In the end, it was simpler than Tammy had expected to escape the big house. When she and Hunter returned inside, they found Freya and Danae had retreated to their room. Armed with the knowledge that the exit was just down the hall through the kitchen, it was an easy matter to convince them to go for a walk outside – although Danae said;

"Are you sure, Tammy? I thought you didn't like walking in the rain." Perhaps she had noticed Tammy's growing aversion to water these last months, after all.

"It's complicated, Mum. But it's nice out there, they have a big garden thing. You'd like it."

"A garden 'thing'? Yes, you're right. I would like that. Come along, Freya. There's nothing to do inside anyway." She picked up her own bag when Tammy took Freya's, and made no further comment.

Outside, Tammy quickly outlined the situation – leaving out her and Freya's dangerous river-crossing yesterday.

"We'd best get back to our house as soon as possible," said Danae. "I doubt anyone else will check on my plants. And I'm sure it's harder to move someone on when they're actually living in a place."

"I'll take you to the edge of our property," said Hunter, who'd accompanied them outside. "Just in case we come across Uncle Archie."

Diana's report had been accurate. There *was* mud everywhere, sticky and dank. The rain eased as they walked, and the thin sunshine warmed the mud and made it release more stench.

"You know, if it weren't for the footprints, this stink would be helpful," Hunter said. "It's hard to smell anything else."

Tammy looked behind them. They had reached the edge of the previously flooded area a few minutes ago, and their trail through the mud was painfully obvious.

"It's not like we're being hunted, though," she said.

Hunter looked at her.

"Isn't it?"

"I'll leave you at the edge of the river," Hunter said. "Maybe you should wade in the water, just at the edge, for a few minutes. Just in case. I'll go over your trail here."

Danae gave Hunter a flat look.

"What is it you're not telling us, young man?"

Hunter didn't quite meet her eyes.

"My Dad's got some unusual ideas," he said. "It's probably best if you're able to leave town for a bit."

"I'd like to know how – or why - we're supposed to achieve that!" Danae exclaimed indignantly.

Hunter was silent.

They reached the river a few minutes later, without seeing Uncle Archie the constable, although there was some barking in the distance. Taking off her shoes, Danae waded in without a backward glance. Freya and Tammy stopped to remove their own shoes. Hunter put his hand on Tammy's arm.

"I really am sorry, you know. I wish it had worked out differently."

Impulsively, Tammy gave him a hug, feeling her damp jacket squish against his rain-frosted wool sweater.

"Never mind. In another lifetime, maybe," she said.

She let him go, picked up her shoes and waded into the muddy river, being careful to stay near the edge. No sense in slipping in. Without that coat, she shouldn't change into anything weird. But the water felt wonderful, whispering over her feet, hinting of untold tales that Tammy could share.

This is more like what a water-goddess should feel. I'm going to have to find out more about those water deities Mum was talking about.

In front of Tammy, Freya half-turned to call back.

"Thanks, Hunter!"

Tammy rolled her eyes.

The yellow hazard tape drooped all along the front of the row of houses that contained their own. Tramping up to their front door, Danae lifted it disdainfully.

"I see no reason for us not to inhabit our own home," she said. "Besides, I couldn't stand staying in that big house another moment. The smell of dogs was unbelievable."

Tammy and Freya looked at each other. Tammy giggled.

"They did have quite a few dogs, yes," she said.

Inside, everything on the ground floor was coated with mud.

"The flood really did reach here," said Freya.

"It appears *that* much of what they told us was true, certainly," said Danae. "This is going to be difficult to clean up."

"They might have had a point about it not being liveable," Tammy muttered.

CHAPTER NINE

Tammy was glad to go to school on Monday. It took her away from the stench and the cleaning frenzy that Danac was directing. Crossing the river was easy now that the flood waters had receded – although several large logs still prevented cars from crossing the bridge, two girls on foot had no trouble. On the other side, Tammy found her bag snagged on a protruding branch. She took care not to be seen as she returned through the mud-slicked gardens. The bag itself was sodden, along with the schoolwork inside. But at least the bag would dry out and be salvageable. She found herself wondering what Hunter had done with his selkie coat. She supposed she'd never know. Not that she wanted it, of course.

Passing the tumbledown house, which was now even more ramshackle, and missing some of its rubbish bags, Freya tugged on Tammy's sleeve.

"I can hear whining again," she said.

Tammy considered. What were the chances an animal around here was a were? Probably quite high. Nevertheless, after a moment, she nodded.

"We'd better go check. Just in case."

After all, it's not raining, and it's not like I'm in that much of a hurry to get to school, where I'll no doubt have to see Hunter again.

Tammy led the way down the overgrown path. She hadn't gone far when she was nearly bowled over by Diana, Hunter's sister – in dog form again. Diana whined frantically, then dashed back down the path.

"It must have been Diana whining," Freya said.

Tammy brushed uselessly at the muddy pawprints on her uniform.

"If I ever do get a dog, it's going to be better trained than that," she said, before following in Diana's trail.

"What would you do with a dog, Tammy? You'd have to take it for walks in the rain," Freya said.

"That'd be alright. I don't mind the rain anymore," Tammy said.

"But I thought..."

"Things change, Freya. Get over it."

A short way down the path, they encountered Diana again, wagging her tail furiously – and standing beside Hunter. Tammy stopped in the middle of the path, blocking Freya, who uttered a wordless protest before she saw who was there.

"What are you doing here, Hunter?" Tammy asked.

He shuffled his feet.

"I just wanted to make sure that you'd made it home alright."

Tammy spread her arms wide.

"You see me alive and well. Satisfied?"

"Yes. Well. I thought I should warn you that Uncle Archie will be probably coming round to your house later. He was muttering about people living in unsafe properties at breakfast, and Dad egged him on. Um."

Tammy snorted.

"I can't believe your family. But I don't know what you expect me to do with that info. I mean – it's not something I can work with. My parents hold the rental, not me."

"Will we be safe?" Freya asked Hunter.

Hunter shrugged helplessly.

"I just thought you should know. Diana and I had to slip out this morning – Dad's forbidden us to go to school until things are cleaned up. We had to swim across the river so no-one in the extended family saw us."

"Well done you. Anything else you have a burning urge to share, while you're performing daring escapes?"

Hunter's face coloured, but he set his jaw.

"That was all."

"In that case, I'd better get Freya to school. I'll tell Mum about your uncle. Later."

"Isn't telling Mum about this more important than school, Tammy?" Freya asked.

"Mum's already gone to work. Come on."

Tammy turned around and tugged Freya with her, back up the lane. There didn't seem to be much else to do.

The eviction notice came a week later, after a series of increasingly tense visits from Hunter's Uncle Archie. Apologies and so forth from the landlord, but he was no longer able to continue renting to them, damage due to flooding, and so on. Tammy and Freya's Dad, Dion, had returned from his sales trip just two days earlier, delayed by flood damage to the train tracks.

"Not a problem," he said. "This place is clearly not going to be habitable for a while yet, anyway. I saw a cottage for rent in a nice little seaside town in my travels. Close to the railway, lovely sea views. Let's move there."

Danae protested, but further enquiry found that there were no other rental properties available in town just then.

"Rather curious in a town this size," she commented. Eventually, with no alternative, Danae agreed to Dion's plan. They loaded a moving truck with their belongings and left town three days later, without seeing Hunter or his family again. But the morning of their departure, a large, squashy parcel arrived for Tammy. It had no return address. She opened it in her emptied-out room. It contained a note with the words 'In case you need it. Hunter.', and a large fur coat.

THE END

About the Author

Melissa Gunn spent several years pursuing a science career before deciding it would be fun to write fiction as well – though it turns out that there is even more research involved. Luckily, research is one of her favourite things. She enjoys combining facts that seem fantastical with actual fantasy and creating quirky characters with a sense of humour. When she's not trying to figure out how a volcano demigod would problem-solve, she is feeding her family or her backyard menagerie. She also takes photographs of whatever will stand still for long enough (so mostly plants). She has lived all over the world but is now based in New Zealand.

Also by Melissa Gunn

Weather Gods:

Flash Flood

Thunder Snow

Storm Surge

Heat Wave

Woodside Cosy Urban Fantasy:

Divination and Disaster

Seers and Salt

Grimoires and Green Tea

Solstice and Silver Spray

Woodside Dryads Cosy Urban Fantasy

Treescape (First published in Magic and Mystery: A Limited Edition Urban Fantasy Mystery Anthology)

Cityscape

Standalone

Halloween Hunt: Paw Prints and Lucky charms

Short stories & novellas:

A Batch of Thornberry Syrup (in Autumn Tales from Cozy Vales)

Seeds of Hope (in The Independent Fantasy and Sci-Fi Magazine)

Feels Like Heaven (in Aftermath: Stories of Survival in Aotearoa New Zealand)

First Pav on Mars (in Pav Deconstructed, Pavlova Press)

A Gift of Coconuts (in Imagine 2200 2024 collection)

Sweet enough? (in Artificial Sweetener: Tales of AI: 100% Written by Humans)

Hauraki Lament or a Song of Love? (in Tales of the Hauraki Gulf)

A Waitākere Werewolf (in Tales in the Waitākere Ranges)

67